The Misplaced Bears

By Veronica C. Sharpe

Printed in the USA

Dedicated to:

KENNEDY (KEN KEN), TEIGEN, AND BRONX, YOU ARE MY LITTLE BEARS, ALWAYS REMEMBER HONI LOVES YOU. JUST AS YOUR LITTLE NAMESAKES, ALWAYS CHOOSE KINDNESS.

Two days before...

In the middle of the night, a truck is bringing cargo to the zoo.

The head zookeeper is watching the growling Mommy polar bear, only to realize she is not growling...she is crying. Thinking to herself, "Do not cry, we will find your baby."

Awakened by the morning light, the baby polar bear cries for his Mommy. Suddenly he hears a soft little voice, "Why are you crying?" There beside him was a young American black bear. The baby polar bear whimpered, "I can't find Mommy."

It is afternoon and the zoo is full of people. Teigen and Bronx must hide. They heard a voice, "Hey, you two, come over here!"

Suddenly they find themselves with a bigger kind of grizzly...bear, and they were so afraid.

The grizzly bear sweetly said, "My name is Ken Ken." She offered them lunch, and then they all laid down for a nap.

It was so quiet, they woke up. "Thank you, Ken Ken for helping us, but we have to go." Ken Ken said, "If you like, you can stay with me and my family." "Sorry, but we have to go find Bronx's Mommy."

Ken Ken said, "I want to make sure you two are safe, so I'm going too."

As the three new friends walked, they stopped to look at the moon. It seemed so big and low to the ground...that they felt they could reach up and touch it.

Mommy polar bear was also looking up at the same big moon...missing her baby.

Bronx was leaning on Ken Ken, suddenly something falls on top of Teigen's head. The two older bears see something black and white in the tree...a panda bear. "Hi, my name is Charlie, ah...do you want that bamboo?" Rubbing her head, Teigen answered, "No thanks."

The three older bears are happy to meet each other. Charlie notices a sleepy little Bronx and offers his den. Thankfully, they decided to spend the night.

After a yummy breakfast, the trio were about to say goodbye when Charlie decided to go with them. So off they went, a baby polar bear, an American black bear, a grizzly bear, and a panda bear, all different, yes...but the same.

Now, because an American black bear, a grizzly bear, and a panda bear were also missing, the zoo had to be closed.

It was around noontime and Bronx was getting tired and cranky. Teigen, Ken Ken, and Charlie tried their best to calm him, but nothing worked...no hugs, no fruit, no fish, no honey, and certainly no bamboo.

A voice shouted, "BRONXY!"

His friends wondered where he was going.

It was his MOMMY! Bronx runs and jumps into her paws. Seeing this made his new friends so happy.

There all together were the missing baby polar bear, the American black bear, the grizzly bear, and the panda bear! Funny they all seemed to be misplaced...but not really. The zookeepers allowed them to stay together for as long as they wanted. Because it was a wonderful thing to see, a new extended family...different, yes...but the same.

The Beginning!